THE GHOST
OF THE TRENCHES

and other stories from
the First World War

This edition published 2014 by
A & C Black, an imprint of Bloomsbury Publishing Plc
50 Bedford Square, London, WC1B 3DP
www.bloomsbury.com
Bloomsbury is a registered trademark of Bloomsbury Publishing Plc

ISBN 978-1-4729-0787-5

A CIP catalogue for this book is available from the British Library.

Printed and bound by CPI Group (UK) Ltd, Croydon CR0 4YY

1 3 5 7 9 10 8 6 4 2

MIX
Paper from
responsible sources
FSC® C020471

THE GHOST OF THE TRENCHES

and other stories from the First World War

HELEN WATTS & TAFFY THOMAS

A & C BLACK
AN IMPRINT OF BLOOMSBURY
LONDON NEW DELHI NEW YORK SYDNEY

CONTENTS

Dedication

To our children and grandchildren
in the hope that they can enjoy
these stories whilst living in peace,
and that they never have to experience
the horrors of a world war.

"In peace, sons bury their fathers.
In war, fathers bury their sons."

Herodotus (Greek historian, 484BC–425BC)

INTRODUCTION:
WAR STORIES

What is a story, and why do people choose to tell stories and listen to them?

Well, quite simply, a story is a description or retelling of an event that is either real or imagined, told using a set pattern of words or themes and with a beginning, a middle and an end. Ever since people developed speech they have communicated in this way – it is the natural thing to do. Stories preserve the past, reveal the present and are part of the creation of the future. The stories we choose to tell, and the stories we choose to listen to, tell people who we are.

If you asked your grandparents about things they did when they were your age, they would probably tell you in a story. Here is an example:

One day in the 1950s, when I was just a boy, I went to stay with my grandfather, Edward Victor French, on his tiny Somerset farm. I was helping to muck out the barn where my grandfather kept the mare that pulled the plough, when I noticed a tin helmet hanging on a nail on an oak beam. I asked my grandfather about it. He told me that as a young man he had joined the Somerset Yeomanry, who were posted to Gallipoli in 1915, and that the tin helmet had kept him safe all the way through the war.

I asked my grandfather what had happened to his horse while he was away. He replied that the horse had gone to war too, but had also returned safely to that Somerset farm. After that, explained my grandfather, the brave horse enjoyed many happy days of retirement, being cared for by my grandfather's four daughters – one of whom was my mother, Mary Joyce.

Beyond that, my grandfather didn't talk much of his experiences in the war as, he said, the things he saw were so terrible. I do recall him making it clear that he didn't want me to play war games wearing that old tin helmet, although he would never say why.

Storytellers like my grandfather express their feelings within the stories they tell. Young men facing great danger and adventure as soldiers in the First World War, far away from their families and homes, would tell each other stories in their quiet moments. Telling stories helped them to deal with their fears and to try and make sense of the things they were seeing and experiencing. Other stories would give them strength by reminding them of their home country and the family and friends they left behind. Other tales would reassure them that Good must triumph over Evil, as in the stories of Jack and the Giant, or Jack and the Devil, where Jack must always win. The British soldier, often referred to as 'Tommy Atkins', was everybody's 'Jack'.

Everybody has got at least one story to tell, and that's their own story. Of those lucky few who came home from the Great War, everyone returned with a different tale. Most of these contained some element of truth, but sometimes, as they were passed on from one mouth to the next, and one generation to the next, that truth became exaggerated, moulded and blended with increasing amounts of fiction. Legends were born and stories that were once personal became lodged in folklore.

Sadly, the last surviving 'Tommy' of the Great War, Harry Patch, died in 2009, so in writing this collection, we have had to delve through a written archive of those who have long since left us, and draw upon the memories that were passed on to the children, and even grandchildren, of those who served. So as the proverb says, 'if we stand tall it is because we are standing on the shoulders of those that have gone before'.

Taffy Thomas

1: THE GHOST OF THE TRENCHES

This tale is inspired by a ghost story from the American Civil War told by US storyteller Dan Keding. The story features two ideas which are common in legends and folk tales about war. The first involves a soldier, who is setting off to war, being given a gift from a loved one. The gift later saves the soldier's life by deflecting an enemy bullet. The second idea, a scenario in which a soldier talks to a dead comrade, has been immortalised in the poem 'Strange Meeting' by Wilfred Owen, which follows this story.

Among the officers who graduated from the Royal Military Academy at Sandhurst before the war was a particularly handsome young man who caught the eye of a young debutante. As they were both only eighteen years of age, the young couple imagined that they had many long days of courting ahead of them.

However, only weeks after they met, something happened which altered not only their lives but also the lives of everyone around them. The Austrian Archduke, Franz Ferdinand, was assassinated and his murder was used as justification for war. One country after the next stepped up to stand and fight alongside its allies, and within weeks peace in Europe was shattered. The Great War had begun.

Realising that it would not be long before he left for France to fight for his country, the young lieutenant, who felt that he would need some support from home, decided to marry his debutante.

A few months later, on the day before the lieutenant marched his platoon up the gangplank of the troop ship, the newlyweds had a quiet but sad farewell. The young man hugged his wife and gave her a sealed envelope. He told her that she was only to open it if he failed to return safely from the war.

Shedding a tear, she in return gave him a silver hip-flask engraved with a heart, their names in the centre, telling him it was filled with brandy, but that was to be kept for a rainy day. He put the flask in his khaki battledress breast pocket, over his heart.

During the years of fighting that followed, there were many times when the lieutenant, fearing for his life and missing his wife, touched his breast pocket and traced the reassuring outline of the hip-flask with his fingers. But he never opened it or touched a drop of the brandy inside.

Then, not long after his twenty-first birthday, he led his platoon over the top into the horror that was Passchendaele. Half of his men, some of them under the age of eighteen, were butchered in the first hail of German bullets. One bullet slammed into the young lieutenant's chest, denting the silver hip-flask, which deflected it. His wife's gift had saved his life.

Two hundred yards into No Man's Land, the young lieutenant discovered the mortally wounded body of an English corporal in a shell hole. Barely alive, the unfortunate soldier had had part of his face shot away. Nevertheless, he still tried to give the makings of a salute to his superior officer.

The lieutenant knelt by the dying corporal, discovering from his thick Lancashire accent that the dying man was of a Pals regiment: friends who decided to join the army and live or die together. The corporal asked the young lieutenant to stay with him as he was afraid to die alone. Seeing the look in the wounded man's eyes, the senior officer knew that he had to do it, even if it put himself at risk.

The wounded soldier pulled a battered envelope from his pocket and asked the officer to deliver it when he returned to Blighty. Glancing at the envelope, the young lieutenant could see that the address written neatly on the front was of a cottage in a small Lancashire mill town. He assured the dying man that he would take care of it. Then he took the dented, treasured hip-flask from his breast pocket and shared the contents with the corporal, the brandy helping him as his life slipped away.

Some months later on his return to England (one of the lucky ones), the young lieutenant did not forget that he had a promise to a dead comrade to keep. A steam train conveyed him and his kit bag to a small station in Lancashire. Then a long walk saw him standing outside a small cottage. A sharp knock on the door of the cottage, and it was opened by a pale, red-eyed woman who seemed surprised to see him there.

The young officer asked if she was the woman who was named on the envelope, and when she said she was, he handed it to her. She looked at the handwriting, and at once burst into tears. The letter contained her dead husband's last words to her.

She thanked the young officer for taking the trouble to bring her the letter, and asked if he had known her husband well. He told her that he had been there in the last moments of her husband's life, sharing a drink with him on the battlefield at Passchendaele.

The woman stared at the lieutenant, astonished. Then, in a trembling voice, she told him that she had already been informed of her husband's death, and that he had died at Serre, a full year before Passchendaele.

The stunned officer returned to Surrey to pick up his life with his young wife, with a story to tell her and a mystery that he could never solve.

Listening to the tale, the young woman was glad that her gift had saved her husband's life and eased the final moments as another brave soldier lost his. How grateful she was that, unlike the poor widow in Lancashire, she would never need to open *her* envelope.

STRANGE MEETING

by Wilfred Owen (18 March 1893–4 November 1918)

It seemed that out of the battle I escaped
Down some profound dull tunnel, long since scooped
Through granites which Titanic wars had groined.
Yet also there encumbered sleepers groaned,
Too fast in thought or death to be bestirred.
Then, as I probed them, one sprang up, and stared
With piteous recognition in fixed eyes,
Lifting distressful hands as if to bless.
And by his smile, I knew that sullen hall;
By his dead smile, I knew we stood in Hell.
With a thousand fears that vision's face was grained;
Yet no blood reached there from the upper ground,
And no guns thumped, or down the flues made moan.
'Strange friend,' I said, 'Here is no cause to mourn.'
'None,' said the other, 'Save the undone years,

The hopelessness. Whatever hope is yours,
Was my life also; I went hunting wild
After the wildest beauty in the world,
Which lies not calm in eyes, or braided hair,
But mocks the steady running of the hour,
And if it grieves, grieves richlier than here.
For by my glee might many men have laughed,
And of my weeping something has been left,
Which must die now. I mean the truth untold,
The pity of war, the pity war distilled.
Now men will go content with what we spoiled.
Or, discontent, boil bloody, and be spilled.
They will be swift with swiftness of the tigress,
None will break ranks, though nations trek from
progress.
Courage was mine, and I had mystery;
Wisdom was mine, and I had mastery;
To miss the march of this retreating world
Into vain citadels that are not walled.
Then, when much blood had clogged their chariot-
wheels
I would go up and wash them from sweet wells,
Even with truths that lie too deep for taint.
I would have poured my spirit without stint
But not through wounds; not on the cess of war.

Foreheads of men have bled where no wounds were.
I am the enemy you killed, my friend.
I knew you in this dark; for so you frowned
Yesterday through me as you jabbed and killed.
I parried; but my hands were loath and cold.
Let us sleep now...'

2: THE ROCK CLIMBERS

Unpredictable, unforgettable and unparalleled in its beauty, the English Lake District in Cumbria has, over the centuries, inspired generations of writers, storytellers and artists and drawn millions of visitors. In Victorian times, when exploration and adventure were very much admired, the Lake District also became a magnet to rock climbers and mountaineers who relished the opportunity to test their skill, strength and courage by conquering the peaks and summits of mountains like Scafell, Helvellyn and Skiddaw. Lakeland continued to be a popular destination for holiday-makers, walkers and climbers into the early twentieth century.

The outbreak of the First World War in 1914 meant that holidays and recreational fun time became severely limited as people concentrated instead on serving their country. However, the following tale, inspired by the many true stories of sadness and loss, courage and friendship, which came out of the trenches of the First World War, is proof that the love of creating and telling stories, and the passion for exploring the mountains, remained strong in the Lake District throughout the twentieth century, right up to the present day.

Imagine a land of gentle green valleys, where frothy white waterfalls tumble into lakes of crystal clear water.

Now imagine a land of jagged, slate-grey rocks clawing at the sky, where black water oozes from boot-sucking bogs into deep, menacing pools.

Picture these two lands merging into one, and you have in your mind the fells, crags, lakes, peaks, tarns and becks of Lakeland: a living, breathing monster of a landscape whose mood can change in a heartbeat. A place where swirling mists suddenly lift to reveal stunning, panoramic views from mountain summits, and where lakes turn from glittering jewels into dark forbidding depths as the sun slips behind incoming clouds.

Standing guard over Lakeland, like three giant kings, are the peaks known as Scafell, Skiddaw and Helvellyn. Soaring the highest of all England's mountains, they have sent out a challenge to climbers and explorers far and wide, over many generations. Who would be brave enough to tackle their steepest ascents? Who could tame the greatest number of peaks?

Among the climbers and explorers who rose to their challenge were two young men who loved to test their skill, strength and courage on the mountains' rocky faces. The two friends grew up together in one of Lakeland's most picturesque villages, and would head for the hills whenever they could. Together, they walked route after route and climbed one rock face after another, until they became accomplished mountaineers.

Lakeland's peaks could be breathtakingly beautiful, but they could also be unforgiving and unpredictable and there was many a time when, had they not been together, one of the pair might have perished. A slip on a razor-sharp scree slope. A booted foot losing its grip off a rain-soaked ledge. A narrow path along a knife-edge suddenly disappearing from view in a dense, descending mist. These and many more dangers had they overcome together. They shared their successes too, as one by one a new pinnacle was reached, a new summit crowned.

And so a bond of friendship was fastened securely between them.

Then the day came when a cloud descended over Lakeland's fells and valleys – a dark, threatening cloud, brought in not by the wind, but by the threat of oncoming war. News of the assassination of an Austrian Archduke; of countries promising to stand together and abide by existing treaties while others declared war on their enemies. Germany invaded Belgium and advanced towards France, and Britain entered the fray. Brave men who once dreamed of conquering Scafell, Skiddaw or Helvellyn now headed for the Western Front.

Out of posters slapped hastily on walls, Lord Kitchener's finger pointed at potential recruits, and the message of 'Your country needs you' reached everyone, even the two companions in their remote Lakeland village.

As a young farmer, who could provide his countrymen with much-needed food, one of the friends remained at home, while the other answered his nation's call and headed for France, Belgium, and the horrors of trench warfare.

Every weekend, the companion who stayed behind would still head for the hills and climb their jagged rocks. But all the while, his thoughts were with his friend. No longer did the views from the mountain tops fill him with joy. No longer did he celebrate reaching a new summit. Climbing without a partner was lonely and full of risk, as any solo climber knows. But the young farmer knew of no other way to pass the time, and so he continued, as the months passed and summer turned to winter, winter to spring, and then spring into summer again.

Then one sunny day, after completing a particularly tough scramble to the top of Scafell Crag, the young man was walking back down through the pass known locally as Hollow Stones when he heard cheery whistling. His heart leaped. Coming towards him he saw the smiling face of his soldier friend, presumably home on leave and heading up on the outward leg of the route he had himself just conquered.

The friends exchanged smiles, delighted to be reunited. They rested for a while, perching on a moss-covered rock, their faces turned up to the warm sunshine, and chatted of what they might do when the war was over.

At last the soldier pointed to the top of the mountain. Understanding his friend's desire to reach the summit before the end of the afternoon when the light would begin to fade, the young farmer stood up and brushed the moss from his trousers. As they parted, the two companions agreed to meet up again that evening for a pint of ale at the Wasdale Head Inn.

The farmer waited patiently in the inn all evening. But the soldier never showed up for that drink.

Anxious that, climbing alone, the soldier had slipped and fallen on one of Scafell's rocky paths, the young farmer set out at first light the next day and combed the hillsides, looking for his friend, until the last drops of daylight were squeezed out of the sun.

The soldier was nowhere to be found.

A couple of days later, at the end of a long day spent rounding up his flock on the fellside, the young farmer received a telegram. His friend had fallen in the Battle of Passchendaele on Belgium's rain-soaked fields, at exactly the time that the pair had met on the mountain in the beautiful sunshine of that Lakeland summer.

The young farmer never told a soul about meeting his friend out on the path at Hollow Stones that day. He was sure no one would believe him. He wasn't sure if he believed it himself. But those who share a love of the mountains and follow the paths that lead up amid Lakeland's more remote pikes and fells are often aware of experiencing there an abiding sense of spirituality – a sense that they are closer, somehow, to the heavens.

Perhaps one day, if you follow the young friends' footsteps and visit those Lakeland fells, you will feel it too.

26

3: The Mysterious Monk

In Slovenia, near the Italian border, lies the picturesque town of Kobarid. The Italians know it as Caporetto and, during the Great War, the town lay right on the Austro-Italian Front. From 24 October to 19 November 1917, Caporetto was the site of a gruelling battle in which the Italian army suffered a heavy defeat at the hands of the Austro-Hungarian and German armies. So great was the Italians' loss that thereafter they used the word caporetto to describe a terrible defeat. The Italian retreat from the Battle of Caporetto became the subject of A Farewell to Arms, *a novel by the American writer Ernest Hemingway. It is also the inspiration for the following legend.*

The story features an Italian monk named Padre Pio. Born in 1887, Padre Pio studied for the priesthood in the friary of St Francis of Assisi and took his final vows in 1907. It is said that at the age of 31, in the year

1917, he collapsed in pain while praying in church. He was found, unconscious, with wounds in his hands and feet and in his side: wounds which matched those of Jesus Christ when he was crucified. There are other people in history, on whose bodies such marks – known as stigmata *– are rumoured to have appeared without cause. Some people believe that they are heaven-sent and are a sign of a devoted Christian believer.*

The appearance of stigmata was not the only miracle associated with Padre Pio. Many people also believed that he had the power to provide miracle cures. Others even claimed that he could appear in two places at once.

Whether or not Padre Pio was really capable of such miracles, he remained in the service of God all his life and built up a loyal following. When he died in September 1968, there were many who argued that he should be made a saint. In 2002, their wish finally came true, when Padre Pio was canonised by Pope John Paul II.

There are many stories told about Padre Pio's life, and many of them, like the one which follows, blend truth with aspects of myth and legend.

It was the night of 24 October 1917, and the soldiers in the Italian army protecting the front line at the foot of the Julian Alps were trying to catch some badly-needed sleep. As they strained their eyes in the dark night, anxious to spot any movement from the enemy, the look-outs lifted their collars to try to keep out the damp and blew on their hands to try to keep out the cold. But all was still.

Midnight came and went and the first few minutes of the new day ticked by. One... two... three... each second echoed by the raindrops which dripped from the butts of the look-outs' machine guns as they maintained their aim across the battlefield and into the drizzly air.

Then suddenly, on the stroke of 2am, there was a boom and a crack, followed by a rush of air. A shower of earth and metal rained down on the look-outs and covered the sleeping Italians in a blanket of dust and dirt.

There were screams, shouts. A whistle blew. The Italian soldiers scrambled to their knees, their heads still fuzzy from sleep, their senses disoriented by the suddenness of the attack. They called to the look-outs, desperate to know where the artillery barrage was coming from, but the early morning mist cloaked their German attackers and made them impossible to track.

And the worst was still to come.

Just when the Italians thought that the artillery barrage had ended, there came another crack, louder this time, like a giant firework, followed by an explosion.

'Gas!' screamed their commander, Luigi Cadorna, as a choking, acid-green smoke crept, assassin-like, along the front line.

The soldiers fumbled in the dark for their gas masks, some already heaving and spluttering as the chemicals burned their throats and filled their eyes and noses; others hopelessly aware that their outdated masks would offer little protection from the deadly fumes.

In total disarray, the Italians gave no counter-fire as the Germans and Austro-Hungarians attacked. The night became day and one after the other, the Italian soldiers fell, and by the time it was night again, their front line was ragged and torn. Disheartened and scared, the men longed for the presence of their revered and respected commander, General Capello, who, at the very time when his leadership was most needed, was confined to his bed with a fever. Hearing of his men's plight and anxious to protect them from further losses, the general ordered them to retreat to the river.

But his command was never carried out, for General Cadorna, who had taken his sick comrade's place, thought he knew better. He demanded that the men regroup and stand their ground, refusing to accept that they were beaten.

Five more days of suffering passed, with the Italians under heavy attack, before the stubborn Cadorna gave the order to retreat. Even then, after witnessing ten thousand of their comrades slaughtered, and three times as many wounded, the battered and exhausted Italians still faced a four-day struggle to cross the river to safety, with the enemy still snapping at their heels.

As the scale of his army's losses – and his responsibility for them – began to hit home, General Cadorna retreated to his tent. Dejected and ashamed, he paced back and forth as he went over and over his mistakes in his mind. He had hoped to make his mark, to lead his men in a reversal of fortune, yet he had ignored the fact that there were not enough mobile reserves to allow any counter-attack to pack a punch. He had cast aside the advice of the best general in Italy and let his ambition and his pride rule his head. If his men had disliked him before, they must surely hate him now. How could he live with himself?

In despair, the commander sank down into his chair and reached for his pistol. Trembling, he held its cold and deadly nose against his head.

But just as he began to put pressure on the trigger with his index finger, there appeared before him a young man dressed in monk's robes. The man held up his hand and spoke sharply to the commander. 'Don't be so foolish!' Then he bowed his head and backed away, disappearing through the folds of the tent.

General Cadorna's hand dropped to his side and the pistol dropped to the floor. Never again, he promised himself, would he contemplate taking his own life, for surely the monk must have been sent from God. Saved by the appearance of the mysterious monk, General Cadorna knew what he had to do. He resigned from his post, leaving active military matters in the hands of wiser men, and secured himself a safer seat on the Allied military council.

Years later, back in his homeland after the war, the General saw the monk once again. This time he was in the beautiful town of San Giovanni Rotondo in the Gargano Mountains of Central Italy. He was visiting a church there when he saw the monk standing by the altar.

The monk recognised the General and spoke to him in the same clear, firm voice that he had used in the tent near the battlefield. He told the commander that his name was Padre Pio, and reminded him about his lucky escape.

The General thanked the monk for saving his life, said a small prayer, and then went on his way.

It wasn't until some days later, when asking after Padre Pio among the inhabitants of San Giovanni Rotondo, that the General learned a startling fact. The monk, he was told, had never once left his friary in the Italian mountains throughout all the years of the Great War.

4: MY DAD'S GOT A GUN

This short tale was given to us by the Cotswold singer and storyteller Ken Langsbury. He heard it from another Gloucestershire folk singer called Bob Bray. Although Ken told it as a Second World War story, we believe that it first surfaced in the Great War of 1914–18 and was recycled when Britain went to war once more in 1939.

Young Tommy's dad didn't go to war. According to Tommy, his mother wrote to the War Office and said that if they took his dad off to war, there would be nobody there to work the horse and then they would all starve. They had a letter back from General Haig himself, saying that he didn't want the country to starve so indeed it *would* be best if Tommy's dad stayed home and worked the horse.

Young Tommy didn't mind his dad not going to war because he couldn't abide fighting, unlike some of the kids at school. One day, one of these warlike kids stood up in the corner of the school playground. With all the little-uns sitting all around him, the big lad boasted, 'My dad's got a gun.'

'Cooorrr!' said all the little-uns. 'Your dad's gotta gun!'

'Yes, my dad's got a gun. He keeps it in a box with his medals.'

The little-uns said, 'Cooorrr! Your dad's gotta gun and he keeps it in a box with his medals!'

They asked young Tommy what his dad had got. Blushing, Tommy answered, 'Nothing.'

The big lad sneered and said, 'Nothing? That's 'cause he's a yellow-bellied coward!'

Angry at his dad being called such a thing, Tommy thought hard. 'No, wait. My dad's got an old army great-coat.'

'Cooorrr!' said all the little-uns. 'Tommy's dad's got an old army great-coat!'

Feeling stronger, Tommy told them that the coat had got a brass button on it.

Impressed, the little-uns said, 'Cooorrr! Tommy's dad's got an army great-coat with a brass button on it!'

They asked Tommy where he kept it.

'He keeps it in the attic, over the tank,' replied Tommy, sticking out his chest with pride.

The little-uns leapt up. 'Cooorrr! Tommy's dad's gotta tank!'

The big lad went quiet and sloped off.

5: An Army of Angels

'The Angels of Mons' is one of the best-known legends of the First World War. Many different versions exist, but it is within the most famous telling of the tale that the origins of the legend lie. For it appears that the idea of angels appearing on the battlefield at Mons originated as a short fictional story called 'The Bowmen', written by Welshman Arthur Machen and published in a London newspaper in September 1914. Machen never claimed his story was true, but the style in which he wrote it was so believable that readers became convinced that it was based on eyewitness accounts. What happened next was an example of how a story can grow and evolve as it is repeated and retold over time. What starts as fiction becomes fact and rumours of strange happenings start to spread. What starts as fact becomes twisted, exaggerated and blended with increasing amounts of fiction.

The historical event that led Arthur Machen to write 'The Bowmen' was the Battle of Mons, which took place from 22 to 23 August 1914. The battle offered the soldiers of the British Expeditionary Force (BEF) their first taste of combat on the Western Front and it proved to be an unforgettable start to the war for them. The action took place near the Belgian town of Mons, close to the border with France. The Allies hoped to hold back the German army and keep them from advancing into French territory. However, the German army proved to be far stronger than the BEF expected, outnumbering the British troops by more than two to one. Losing the support of their French allies, who withdrew towards Paris, the British were heavily defeated and were forced into a rapid retreat.

As they stared into the jaws of defeat, it is probable that some of the British soldiers, exhausted and terrified, called upon friendly spirits and saints to come to their aid, and it is not unlikely that they may have seen strange visions or experienced hallucinations. Whatever the truth, after Arthur Machen's fictional story was published, several soldiers came forward and claimed to have seen angels or phantoms on the battlefield at Mons. A story which was first written as pure fiction, then dismissed as a deliberate hoax, began *to evolve into a wartime legend. The retelling of the legend of the Angel of Mons that follows is inspired by Arthur Machen's original story.*

Among the hundred thousand brave soldiers who made up the British Expeditionary Force at the start of the Great War was a sharp-eyed Londoner named Charlie. Charlie was blessed with a beautiful singing voice and as a young boy had dreamed of a career on the stage. But a life treading the boards was no life at all, said his grey-haired father, who promptly sent his son off to volunteer for the Territorial Army.

A bright student and a quick learner, Charlie soon proved himself to be a skilled marksman. His friends called him Crack-shot Charlie, and when he was ready to be sent all the way to Africa and the Boer War, his nickname travelled with him.

So by the time August 1914 came around, when the British Expeditionary Force was boarding the ferry for France, Charlie was already an accomplished soldier. Brimming with confidence, he led a rousing rendition of the song 'It's A Long, Long Way To Tipperary', as his battalion disembarked and marched south to the Belgian border, the men swinging their arms and stepping out in time to the tune.

It's a long way to Tipperary,
It's a long way to go.
It's a long way to Tipperary,
To the sweetest girl I know!
Goodbye Piccadilly,
Farewell Leicester Square!
It's a long, long way to Tipperary,
But my heart's right there.

As the men drew closer to the front line near Mons, they heard stories of the Belgian city's links with England's patron saint George, who had slain the mythical dragon.

'They still slay dragons here,' remarked a young corporal named Lewis, as he described the great feast which was held every year in Mons in the saint's memory, in which replicas of the dragon were put to the sword. 'I pray to God that we can slay our enemy just as easily,' he added, thinking of the great German army which was gathering nearby, trying to push its way onto French land.

Charlie and his battalion did not have long to wait to feel their own dragon's hot breath on their skin. The following morning, they heard news that their cavalry, leading the BEF's advance and some distance ahead, had spotted the enemy.

Letting out a thunderous roar, the cavalrymen drew their swords and charged, proud to be leading their country into the Great War. Their enthusiasm served them well, for the British horsemen took many German lives and led away a band of sorry German prisoners.

Meanwhile back at Mons and under the watchful eye of Commander Haig, Charlie and his battalion had dug themselves a thin line of trenches along the banks of a moss-green canal, hoping that its slow-moving waters would offer some protection when the fighting began.

As night fell and the men tried to snatch some precious hours of sleep, Charlie eased their path into slumber by softly singing some lines from their favourite Tipperary tune:

Up to mighty London came
An Irish lad one day,
All the streets were paved with gold,
So everyone was gay!
Singing songs of Piccadilly,
Strand, and Leicester Square,
'Til Paddy got excited and
He shouted to them there...

At first light the next morning, Charlie and his fellow soldiers awoke to find everything around them soaked in a depressing, dank drizzle. Like a smothering blanket, a thick mist clung to the surface of the canal and remained there way into the morning, making any attempt at attack sheer madness.

Frustrated, the men lay staring over the muddy lip of the trench into the swirling white, and even Charlie remained silent, holding back his songs for better times.

At one point, the first gust of wind of the morning lifted the edge of the foggy blanket and exposed the British lines to the eyes of a nervous German sniper across the canal. His finger jerked on the trigger of his rifle and the sound of his premature gunshot spread panic among the rest of the men in his dugout, who instantly opened fire too.

Their experience of warfare kept Charlie and his battalion confident and calm. They remained still, with their heads down low, letting the wild rush of bullets whistle over their heads rather than trying to fire back blindly across the water. Saving his ammunition, Charlie replied to the gunfire with song, loudly chanting some more lines from his favourite tune before silence fell across the canal once more.

Paddy wrote a letter
To his Irish Molly O',
Saying, 'Should you not receive it,
Write and let me know!
If I make mistakes in spelling,
Molly dear,' said he,
'Remember it's the pen, that's bad,
Don't lay the blame on me.'

Eventually, as the morning hours passed and the sun climbed higher in the sky, it burned the remaining mist off the ground and the drizzle dried up.

'Holy smoke!' exclaimed Lewis as he could see for the first time the true scale of the beast they were about to fight. 'There's twice as many of them as us.' He tightened his grip on the barrel of his gun.

Before Charlie could reply, the German artillery barrage began, raining down on the British trenches from higher ground. In its wake came a second wave of attack, this time at ground level, as hundreds of German infantry men poured across the canal's narrow bridges, while others clambered across lock gates to get closer to their enemy.

It was time for Charlie to live up to his nickname and, breathing steadily, he began to pick off one German after the next, never missing a target. Each time a bullet found its mark, he celebrated with another line from the Tipperary tune.

'Crack-shot! Over there! Look!' screamed Lewis, pointing to a brave German soldier who had swum across the canal and was now frantically winding the mechanism to close the swing bridge.

Charlie hit him with his first shot, but it was too late. The swing bridge was closed. The Germans now had an even easier route across the water. The machine gunners posted along the British lines continued to blast away at the approaching enemy, but for every group of grey-uniformed men who fell, another would replace it.

The British were being overwhelmed.

Perhaps Charlie and the BEF would have stood a better chance if their allies had stood firm alongside them. But having suffered heavily already as the Germans advanced through Belgium, the French were rushing back instead to defend their beloved Paris, and so the British force was left exposed on both sides.

As morning turned into afternoon, the Germans started to pick off the British machine gun posts. One by one, the British guns were silenced and the Germans sniffed their first whiff of victory. With no machine gun fire to cut them down, they now came crashing down into the British trenches, forcing Charlie and his comrades to fight at close range. Brutal and bloody, the gruelling battle raged until nightfall.

As the sky turned black, Charlie looked about him and shivered, realising that his battalion was surrounded. Tipping his Tommy helmet to young Lewis, who had been fighting bravely at his side, Charlie's voice cracked as he sang the third line of his song:

Goodbye Piccadilly,
Farewell Leicester Square!

But Lewis did not join in with the refrain. He shook his head, refusing to give up, for he was remembering the prayer he had said when the battalion arrived in Mons. 'Adsit Anglis Sanctus Georgius!' the young corporal cried out in Latin, calling upon Saint George to make himself present and help them.

As soon as Lewis had uttered his plea, Charlie felt his skin turn icy cold and he could see his breath, heavy on the night air. He looked up and to his amazement a shaft of bright light suddenly penetrated the night sky, like sunlight creeping through a tear in a blackout curtain, and the battlefield was illuminated in a ghostly glow.

Then floating down the beam of light came a host of silver-white angels, dressed as archers and carrying golden bows and arrows. Like the mist which had hovered over the canal that dawn, the angels floated above the ground between the two armies' lines and spread their glistening wings to shelter Charlie and the remaining British soldiers from harm.

Charlie stood in awe, rooted to the ground as he watched one angel raise its hand and point at the enemy. The entire army of angels took aim and released their bowstrings, showering the Germans with shimmering arrows and pinning them back so that Charlie and his comrades could make their retreat.

Charlie and his companions fled south from Mons, only slowing to an exhausted trudge when the cries of battle behind them had completely faded away. No one spoke a word.

Those who had witnessed the heavenly bowmen were unsure whether or not to believe what they had seen. Others kept shaking their heads as if trying to clear their minds of a temporary madness. Many more were too traumatised by the scale and the speed of their defeat in the battle to utter a sound. Some were so tired that they slept as they walked.

When they finally halted and were given permission to rest, dawn was already breaking. As the sun crept above the horizon, Charlie dropped down onto the damp grass alongside Lewis. 'Was that just the mist coming down again, playing tricks on our eyes, or did we really see an army of angels back there?'

'Oh, we saw angels all right,' Lewis replied. 'Saint George answered my call.'

Charlie didn't reply. Instead he tilted his face upwards, looking questioningly at the sky, but all was still. Then he lay down on his back, covering his eyes with his hat, and began to sing under his breath...

It's a long way to Tipperary,
It's a long way to go.
It's a long way to Tipperary,
To the sweetest girl I know!
Goodbye Piccadilly,
Farewell Leicester Square!
It's a long, long way to Tipperary,
But my heart's right there.

6: The Mysterious Case of the Extraordinary, Exploding Ships

When the 15,000-ton battleship HMS Bulwark *exploded while moored up at Sheerness in Kent, at the mouth of the River Medway on 26 November 1914, just a few months after the outbreak of the war, no one was quite certain of the cause. With no enemy in sight, and no sign of attack on this great ship anchored in the apparent shelter of home waters, even the Admiralty's Official Commission of Inquiry had to admit that the actual cause might never be discovered. And that might have been that. Case closed...*

Until it happened again.

On the morning of 26 November 1914, the British battleship HMS *Bulwark* was moored in the mouth of the River Medway. The water was calm and the last of her crew had just climbed on board after spending a restful day's leave in the nearby Kent town of Sheerness.

At 7.35am, everything changed. As the men sat in the mess enjoying their breakfast, the entire ship began to rumble and then, with a huge roar, she exploded in a flash of flame which burst up through the decks and tore the vessel violently apart.

By the time the smoke from the explosion had cleared, HMS *Bulwark* had sunk beneath the dark, murky waters, with only fourteen of her 750 crewmen left alive.

No one could explain why the great battleship had exploded and although two inquests were held, a verdict of accidental death was returned and the case was closed.

Just over a year later, on 30 December 1915, a sea captain named Eric Back was refusing to let the Great War dampen his festive spirits and was entertaining his officers and their families on board the armoured cruiser HMS *Natal*. While his ship was peacefully at anchor along with the rest of its fleet in Scotland's Cromarty Firth, he was treating his guests to a film show.

Everyone was in high spirits, excited and delighted to be partying with the captain of such a wonderful modern ship which had already earned itself an impressive reputation. For in 1911, HMS *Natal* had escorted King George V and Queen Mary to their great coronation as Emperor and Empress of India in Delhi.

Indeed, such was the guests' merriment that the sounds of their laughter and cheer leaked from the port-holes and filled the ears of the ship's crew, who were heading ashore for some well-earned leave, and were climbing into a flotilla of small boats ready to travel back to dry land. With the prospect of Hogmanay celebrations ahead, spirits were high in the little boats. Not one of their passengers had any idea that they were about to witness a shocking scene.

At exactly 3.20pm, the entire Firth shook with a tremendous, ear-splitting explosion. Startled and shaken, the crew being carried ashore in the flotilla looked back to HMS *Natal*. The sight they saw was so frightening that, for a moment, no one said a word. Huge flames were shooting up into the sky from the great cruiser's stern.

On board, a brave and capable lieutenant named ˌ had run out onto the quarterdeck, alarmed by the ˌ and expecting to see his ship under enemy attack. But as he scanned the waters around him and looked out to the horizon, the only craft he could see were the tiny boats bobbing about on the waves, taking his fellow crewmen to shore.

Then came a second blast, and Lieutenant Fildes was thrown down onto the deck. His head struck the ground with the force of the explosion and he lay there for a few seconds unable to move. Then, as his senses returned, he realised that the teak deck beneath his hands felt hot to the touch.

He rolled over, still half-dazed, and saw a sight so horrific he was sure it was the work of the devil himself. The wood of the deck was beginning to bubble and boil, turning black in an instant as the flames beneath it set light to the pitch that coated every plank.

From their viewpoint on the small boats, the crew watched the rear decks and gun casements of HMS *Natal* being blown apart. Then, as arguments broke out among them – some screaming that they should return to the cruiser to give help while others shouted that nothing could be done and they were wiser to flee to shore and to safety – HMS *Natal* heeled over to her port side.

Within just three shocking minutes, the glorious HMS *Natal* had sunk to the unforgiving, icy depths of Cromarty Firth, taking more than 350 souls to their deaths.

In the weeks that followed the tragedy, many theories were put forward as to the cause of the sinking of HMS *Natal*. There were those who were convinced that the Germans had somehow managed to hit the cruiser with a torpedo; but a fleet of Allied submarines kept Cromarty Firth well protected and not one crew member on board any of those vessels had spotted an enemy missile.

Then there were those who were sure that the explosion came from inside the great cruiser, suggesting that HMS *Natal* had been blown up by a fault with her own magazines. But as the magazines were kept in the lowest part of the hull and were considered well and safely stored, this idea was also dismissed as unlikely.

Theories about incendiary devices were quashed, too, when Lieutenant Fildes, who had managed to escape in the nick of time from the melting quarterdeck, confirmed that he had thought he had heard a strange crackling noise near the magazine store. But following procedures, he had had the noise investigated and it had proved to be a false alarm.

No one seemed to know for sure what had really happened. There was only one thing which no one could deny: once again, as on the ill-fated HMS *Bulwark,* there had been a mysterious and sudden explosion on board a well-protected ship, away from battle and considered to be safely moored up in home waters.

But at the very least, such a thing could never happen a third time ... or could it?

On 14 July 1917, a fast and seemingly impregnable battleship, the great HMS *Vanguard*, exploded and sank almost instantly while sailing in Scapa Flow in the Orkney Islands. Eight hundred and four lives were lost and only two men survived.

Could it be that German torpedoes had found their mark? Or was it the work of saboteurs? Could either really have escaped the notice of the surrounding craft and crew on three separate occasions?

No one wanted to believe that some sloppy internal error or mistake on board had led to internal explosions on all three ships. But what else might be the cause?

Were the British Naval Authorities as uncertain about the causes of these terrible incidents as they claimed? Perhaps they knew full well, but didn't want to show their hand to their German enemy. Or perhaps ... just perhaps ... there was some other strange force at work.

It seems that the case of the extraordinary, exploding ships may never be solved for certain. And perhaps we should be satisfied to let it rest, along with the rusting physical clues and the hundreds of sleeping eye-witnesses, deep at the bottom of the sea.

7: THE BOY AND THE HARP

Most English churches today have floors made of stone or even marble. However, many years ago, as far back as the Middle Ages, the majority of them would have been far more basic, with simple, earth floors covered with rushes. This created a chilling and a rather smelly problem, because local folk – particularly important ones – who died in the parish were sometimes buried inside the church as well as in the churchyard. With only soil between the worshippers and the rotting corpses beneath their feet, the air inside the church could become less than fragrant in the summer and, in the winter, extremely chilly and damp. So on festival and feast days, it became a tradition for the local people to bring to the church fresh rushes, which would be scattered all over the floor to sweeten the air and help keep the congregation warm and their feet dry. The practice was referred to as Rushbearing.

In the 1800s, when stone floors became more commonplace in churches, the tradition of Rushbearing all but died out. However, five churches – all in Cumbria and St Oswald's of Grasmere among them – held on to the tradition and still maintain it today by holding a procession followed by a special service in the church. In Grasmere, Rushbearing Day is the Saturday which falls the closest to St Oswald's Day, 5 August. In the year of the new Millennium – that is, the year 2000 – that happened to be the saint's day itself.

The following tale focuses on a young Grasmere lad who took part in the Rushbearing procession in the years preceding the First World War.

This story comes from the picturesque Cumbrian village of Grasmere. It involves a boy, a harp, a special village festival and a war that was raging hundreds of miles away from the peace and tranquility of Lakeland. Appropriately, the story begins in a storyteller's garden: a garden belonging to the storyteller Taffy Thomas which happens to be across the road from a church: St Oswald's Church.

One hot August day in the year 2000, the storyteller, who was dressed in a buttercup-yellow waistcoat and a cream Panama hat, was leaning on the dry-stone wall of his garden, watching a procession passing by. The procession had woven its way around the narrow lanes of the village and was now passing his garden and heading for the Church.

Anyone in Grasmere that day who was unfamiliar with the traditions of this Lakeland village might have wondered what on earth was going on, for the people, young and old, who marched in the procession were carrying strange-shaped sculptures crafted from reeds – or rushes – decorated with flowers.

Taffy the storyteller, who had lived in Grasmere for many years, knew that this was Rushbearing Day, a festival which had its roots hundreds of years ago, back in the Middle Ages, when local people walked together to their local church and scattered fresh rushes on the earthen floor, to purify the air and help keep out the cold.

As they passed by, the people in the procession laughed and waved to Taffy, for he and his special storytelling garden were well-known in the community. The storyteller waved back, admiring the rushes, most of which were fashioned into the shape of a cross or some other biblical symbol, such as a basket to represent of the story of the baby Moses set adrift in his makeshift wicker bed on the River Nile.

However, one sculpture carried in the procession that day stood out from the others and caught the storyteller's eye, for the reeds of this sculpture had been twisted into the shape of a harp.

By now, a small crowd had gathered on the narrow pavement on the other side of the garden wall to watch the procession, and if those people were wondering about the significance of this haunting, multi-stringed instrument in the Rushbearing ceremony, the storyteller certainly wasn't. He knew the two people carrying it and he knew their story. Their names were Terry and Sarah O'Neill, and you might recognise their surname as being from Irish heritage. What's more, you might also know that the harp is Ireland's official symbol and has appeared on its coat of arms since medieval times.

But national pride was not the only reason why Terry and Sarah O'Neill were carrying a harp in the procession that summer's day, and as the procession made its way through the church gate, the storyteller began to tell the crowd of onlookers their tale.

'Over a hundred years ago,' began the storyteller, 'there was born in this village a baby boy. His parents named him William – although everyone called him Billy –

and they also gave him the rather grand middle name of Warwick. So his full name was William Warwick Peasecod.'

One of the little girls in the crowd sniggered. 'What a funny name! *Peasecod*!'

'Yes, I suppose it does sound peculiar, but that's only because *peasecod* is a word that has gone out of use today. Once upon a time it was more commonly used to describe the pod of a pea plant.' The storyteller smiled and the little girl smiled back. Then he carried on his tale.

'So where were we? Yes! William, or Billy, as he was known, was born here in Grasmere in 1898. He was a good son and, to his parents' delight, he was gifted with a charming singing voice. So when he was old enough, Billy joined the church choir. He could be found over there,' said the storyteller, pointing to St Oswald's over the road, 'every Sunday morning and sometimes on weekdays too, whenever there was a wedding.

'Billy was among those children who, when they were big enough and strong enough, were chosen to carry the rushes in the annual Rushbearing procession. This caused Billy much excitement and was a matter of great pride to his parents. All they could talk about for days on end was what shape Billy's rushes should be and how they could make the sculpture.

'Then Billy's parents hit on an idea. As their family was of Irish descent, wouldn't it be grand if Billy's rushes were in the shape of a harp? Not only was this the symbol of the beloved land of their fathers, it was also a reference to the Harp of David from the Bible story in which David the shepherd boy – chosen by God to be the future King of Israel – is invited to play the harp for Saul, King of the Israelites. Like Billy, David was musically gifted, and his harp playing was so beautiful that it soothed the anxious king and gave him renewed strength for his forthcoming battle against the Philistines.

'So, having settled on a design, Billy's father went to see the local carpenter and commissioned him to make his beloved son a wooden frame in the shape of a harp. When the frame was ready, Billy's mother went down to the shore of Grasmere to gather some rushes. Then she rowed out into the deep, dark waters of the lake to collect some fresh water-lilies.

'On the eve of Rushbearing Day, Billy's mother worked long into the night, threading the rushes in and out and all around the wooden frame, and weaving the lilies in amongst them. By morning, when Billy came down into the parlour to have his breakfast, the harp was ready.

'Billy's harp was the finest of all the rushes in the procession that day, and his parents were filled with so much joy and pride as they watched their son carrying the harp into the church, that they promised to keep the same wooden frame and decorate it for Billy to carry in the Rushbearing procession every year from that day forwards.

'And they did just that. Every Rushbearing Day, as Billy turned thirteen, fourteen, fifteen and then sixteen, he could be seen alongside his friends and companions in the procession through the village, holding his harp high up in the air and smiling broadly.

'But while the days in Grasmere remained peaceful and calm, life outside the little Lakeland village was far from either of those things, for the Great War had begun, and Lord Kitchener had put out his call for volunteers to fight the Allies' campaign on the Western Front.

'So not long after his seventeenth birthday, in 1915, Billy Peasecod exchanged his harp made of rushes for a standard issue rifle and joined the Border Regiment as a signaller. After saying a tearful goodbye to his mother and father, Billy set off for France.

'It was the signaller's job to send signals and messages back from the fighting to the Company's headquarters, which meant that poor young Billy spent most of his days near the front line in the midst of all the action and, of course, the danger.

'Those long, terrible days in the trenches left Billy feeling a lifetime away from the green valleys and rugged mountains of Lakeland and from his solid, little, slate-grey home, on the edge of the beautiful village, nestled between the River Rothay and the twinkling waters of Grasmere. But like King Saul, who found comfort in David's harp playing before fighting the Philistines, Billy took comfort in his memories of home, of singing alongside his friends in the choir, and of those special days when he would carry his harp in the parade.

'The war raged on. Two Rushbearing Days came and went and, watching the processions back in Grasmere village, Billy's parents dreamed of the day when their son would be back and carrying his harp once again. But sadly their wish would never be fulfilled, for on 5 November 1917, nineteen-year-old Billy was killed on the battlefields of France.

'Although they couldn't bear to part with the harp, Billy's mother and father could not face the thought of anyone carrying it in his place in the Rushbearing procession – not in the year after he died nor in the summers that followed. So gradually the harp fell into disrepair.

'Eventually, Billy's parents grew old and, one after the other, were put to rest in the cemetery at Great Cross at Grasmere. But their story, and that of the harp, and the story of the young choirboy with the beautiful Irish voice who became a soldier, lived on, as one generation of Billy's family passed it down to the next.

'And now I have passed it on to you,' said the storyteller, lifting his panama hat and giving a little bow to his listeners.

A ripple of applause ran round the small crowd. Thanking the storyteller, the people began to disperse, some to follow the procession into the church, others to make their way off around the village to do a little sightseeing.

Only the little girl who had chuckled over Billy Peasecod's name hung back. Tugging on the corner of storyteller's waistcoat, she looked up into his whiskery face and asked: 'But what about those people? The lady and the man who were carrying the harp just now? Who are they?'

'Ah, that's a very good question,' said the storyteller, 'as the answer closes the circle in Billy's tale. They are members of the O'Neill family, Billy Peasecod's relatives. As I said in my story, no one felt that it was right to carry Billy's harp for a very long time after he died, but because it's the Millennium Rushbearing this year, which makes it a very special year, Terry and Sarah O'Neill thought it would be nice to remember Billy. So they had that harp specially made. It's an exact replica of the one Billy had.'

The little girl nodded. 'It's a good story,' she said. 'I liked it. And I think I would have liked Billy too, if I had met him. Is it okay if I tell his story to my friends?'

'Of course,' said the storyteller. 'I think Billy would like that very much indeed.'

We Must Not Forget

The following poem was written in 2012 by war veteran George Harrison of Kirkby Lonsdale, then in his 90th year. George's father and grandfather were both Non-Commissioned Officers (NCOs) in the Territorial Army before the war broke out in 1914. Every Armistice Day, George can be seen standing next to Kirkby Lonsdale's war memorial, reading out the names of local folk who have died at war, many of whom he knew.

I don't think they really knew
That soldiering was not a game,
Target practice was really fun
And marching just the same.
But then there was the horror
Of tanks and gas and flame,
We must not forget those
brave young men
Who came not home again.

8. The Regiment That Vanished

The story that follows, still widely known throughout central Lancashire, explains why the folk in this part of England have never forgotten the kindness of an order of French monks and continue to buy and consume produce from their monasteries as a measure of their gratitude.

It is not the only First World War legend involving vanishing soldiers. There is also a tale about a regiment from Norfolk, known as the Sandringham Pals, who were fighting in Gallipoli in August 1915. The soldiers were seen marching up a hillside into a low-lying mist – but they never came out again. After the war, despite attempts by the British government to trace the missing men, they were never found.

A British regiment known as the Lancashire Fusiliers was pinned down in a shell hole somewhere on the Siegfried Line in northern France. Things were looking grim. They were being picked off, a man at a time, by small arms fire from the German infantrymen in the trench a mere fifty yards opposite.

But that was not their biggest concern. An even bigger worry was the German heavy gun emplacement just beyond that trench. The Fusiliers were well in its sights.

The Lancashire men were not particularly devout Christians, but prayer was their only option. As they prayed, their hands clasped tight, a sixty-pound shell smacked into the mud just in front of their frail refuge. It created a monumental column of black smoke completely engulfing the terrified soldiers, whose only answer was to pray even harder.

Daring to open their eyes, the soldiers were amazed to see several shadowy, robed figures beckoning them. They were sure that their prayers had been answered and these were angels.

Under the cover of the thick black smoke, the Lancashire lads followed their cloaked saviours. It wasn't until they reached the relative safety of a nearby monastery that they realised that the figures who had answered their prayers were, in fact, Benedictine monks. Protected inside the monastery walls, the soldiers and the Benedictine brothers knelt together in prayer.

Back on the battlefield, the tower of black smoke had dispersed. To the amazement of the German gunners, peering down the sites of their great gun for a killer hit, the British regiment they had witnessed being engulfed within it, had completely disappeared.

Along the British line, lookouts also marvelled at the disappearance of a whole regiment, especially as the next heavy shell – a ninety-pounder – smacked straight into the hole where the Lancashire boys had been cornered.

Meanwhile, after precious hours resting in the monastery, where they were treated to both food and drink, the Lancashire Fusiliers prepared to return to the battlefield. Offering thanks and words of farewell to the monks, they marched off boldly, ready to pick up fresh orders.

9: THE PHANTOM SOLDIERS OF CRECY

The battles of the First World War were not the first to be fought on the fields and floodplains of France's River Somme. Plenty more blood had been spilled on this land in the centuries which preceded it. Perhaps the ghosts of those poor souls lost in the past are drawn to those living who face the same dangers and fears as they did; for there are countless stories from the Great War of soldiers seeing ghosts and phantoms of military men – either on the battlefields themselves or in the surrounding villages and countryside. Here is one such tale.

For the town of Wimereux, on the northern French coast, not far south from Calais, the Great War really did live up to its name, for it transformed the town from a small port into a busy military hospital centre. By the end of the war, it even played host to the General Headquarters of the British Expeditionary Force.

And it was to this town that a British staff colonel – a tall, striking, no-nonsense kind of man called Colonel Shepheard – was headed one late March afternoon in 1918. The Colonel was exhausted. His men had endured days of heavy, relentless bombardment in damp, foggy trenches, and even the support of the Australian forces could not hold back the German advance. The German Spring Offensive was taking its toll. So when he was ordered back to HQ for a briefing, the Colonel was secretly glad of the opportunity for a few hours' respite.

As soon as he climbed into the car and his driver and interpreter, Jean-Claude, started the engine, Colonel Shepheard wound down his window, hoping to let the cool air rush over his face and revive him. But the terrible noise of the continuing battle he was leaving behind him still filled the air, and he rapidly closed the window again, feeling both relieved and guilty at being able to shut it out.

He didn't feel like talking, but idle conversation with the Frenchman at his side helped the Colonel to stay awake for the journey north. So, as they passed through village after village, and wound their way to

Wimereux, the pair passed the time sharing stories about their families and their loved ones left at home.

By the time they reached their quarters in Wimereux, the sky was dark. The two men ate a meal together and then, dog-tired, they headed for their beds.

The Colonel was glad of his first comfortable mattress in days and was soon in a deep sleep. Yet though he slept deeply and his tired bones rested, his mind was still active and he had a vivid dream.

The Colonel dreamed of the journey he had made that day with Jean-Claude, retracing the route in his mind, as the car raced along from one village to the next. In his slumber, the Colonel re-lived every detail of his journey, with one significant difference. In his dream, just after the Colonel and his interpreter had passed through one small village, something made them slow down and stop the car. Neither man spoke. Neither one questioned the other. The pair simply stared along the road ahead of them in silence, watching and waiting.

Then suddenly, out of the ground along either side of the road, rose thousands of ghostly figures. Each was wearing a silver-grey cloak with a hood pulled over his head. Some were carrying spears, others swords, but all held their weapons down, hanging limply at their sides. Although the phantoms did not move, nor make a sound, they shimmered in the dusk, like wisps of smoke in the gloomy air, and yet at the same time their shape, colour and form was clear.

To his surprise, the Colonel found that he was calm and not at all afraid. Quietly, without a word to his driving companion, he stepped out of the car and began to walk slowly, up and down between the two lines of ghostly men.

Still the figures made no noise, but as his gaze fell upon them, each phantom fixed its ghostly eyes on the Colonel and stared at him. The Colonel was overcome with a sense of sadness, for there was no anger in these silvery soldiers' eyes, only sorrow and pain.

The Colonel took a step towards one of the phantoms and reached out his hand to touch the edge of his cloak, but as soon as his fingers made contact with the luminous fabric...*puff*...it disintegrated into a silvery powder that floated down to his feet. It was as if his touch had broken a spell, for at that instant, every single one of the thousands of phantom soldiers simultaneously turned into dust and disappeared back into the earth from which he had sprung.

When he woke the next morning, the Colonel remembered every detail of the dream and try as he might, he was unable to shake it from his mind. Over breakfast, he found himself sharing the details of his vision with his interpreter. Would the Frenchman think that the Colonel had gone mad, perhaps, and that the horror of battle had corrupted his mind?

Not at all. For the interpreter listened intently, then when the Colonel had finished, he asked him about the village near where, in the dream, they had stopped the car.

The Colonel did his best to describe the small village which he had now passed through twice – once on his real journey the day before, and once in his dream. He remembered a small cross or monument made from stone and red-brick, and driving by a beautiful yet unusual church with both a bell tower and a watchtower.

The Frenchman took a sip of his coffee then nodded his head as he swallowed. 'Without doubt,' he said, 'the village you are describing to me is Crécy, and the vision you have seen in your dream is not unknown to me. There are many others who have witnessed a similar sight. Your sleep has been invaded by the ghosts of the bowmen who died in the Battle of Crécy over 570 years ago.'

The Frenchman told his companion all about the famous battle which took place at Crécy in 1346, during the Hundred Years War, when King Edward III's army, although massively outnumbered by its French enemy led by Philip VI, was eventually victorious.

The English owed their victory to their shrewd tactics, fighting on foot from a strong, defensive position on high ground. Fatigued from days of marching, the French crossbowmen, who marched at the front of the army, were at a major disadvantage. Their bows were wet and ineffective and they were fighting without the usual protection of their shields.

Aware that his men were suffering heavy casualties, it was not long before the French leader ordered his army's retreat and the English declared a decisive victory.

At once the Colonel understood the pathetic, defeated look he had seen in the eyes of the phantoms that had lined his route in his dream. He understood, too, why the presence of an English military man, crossing their ancient, bloody resting place, might summon the spirits of an old French enemy, long since dead.

10: SERGEANT STUBBY

Have you ever heard someone describing a dog as 'man's best friend'? It is a well-used phrase because it sums up perfectly the companionship between people and domestic dogs, and the loyalty and love that dogs show towards their owners. Yet dogs can be more than just good friends. They can also be a source of practical help and support. Today, dogs carry out a range of jobs – from guiding the blind and assisting the disabled to rounding up sheep and sniffing out drugs and explosives.

During World War I, there were thousands of working dogs who more than lived up to the name of 'man's best friend'. One of their most important jobs involved carrying messages to and from the trenches. Dogs could run faster than human messengers across ground which was often difficult, rough and muddy. Because they could move more quickly, it was harder for enemy snipers to spot and shoot them.

Dogs were also employed to listen for – and sniff out – wounded soldiers, or enemies hiding in underground tunnels. Others were trained to pull along supply carts.

Many of the dogs who went to war were much loved by the soldiers in the trenches. They offered comfort and companionship, especially to those who were homesick, wounded or dying.

The following tale is inspired by one very special dog who went to France during the Great War. No one knows for sure where the truth about his adventure starts and ends, but the brave little dog has become a war legend on both sides of the Atlantic.

If you are ever fortunate enough to travel to America and visit the neighbourhood of Georgetown in the capital city of Washington DC, you will discover that this is a university town, and if you look closely at the hats, T-shirts and hoodies that the athletics students wear, you will see that they bear the symbol of a bulldog.

This is not just a symbolic animal image, like the speedy jaguar or the galloping horse used by famous car manufacturers, or the leaping springbok that the South African rugby team wears on its shirts. No, this is a real dog, a hero who became a legend, and his name was Stubby.

In fact, Stubby was not a bulldog at all. He was what we call a cross-breed: half Boston terrier and half bull terrier, and considering that he became world-famous, this little dog's life began very differently to how you might imagine. For when he was a puppy, Stubby was either abandoned or lost by his owners. Alone, hungry and thirsty, the poor little pup found himself wandering the streets of New Haven in the American state of Connecticut.

Goodness knows what he went through during those tough first days of his life. Perhaps he had to learn very quickly how to react to danger. Perhaps he had to set aside his fears and learn to be brave. But whatever he saw, whatever he did, the little dog learned how to survive.

One day, while trotting along a street in the city, the little stray wandered onto the edge of a baseball field where a group of soldiers from the nearby military camp were training. They were being drilled ready to leave for the Great War, thousands of miles over the ocean in Europe.

Tired from his wanderings, the stray dog lay down in the shade of a tree. He rested there all afternoon, watching the soldiers going through their paces. One of the soldiers, a corporal named Robert Conroy, had spotted the dog and was watching him out of the corner of his eye. Every time his drill sergeant turned away, Corporal Conroy would cast a glance to the side of the field to see if the little dog was still there. He wondered where he came from and who he belonged to, for he had never seen him there before.

When the whistle finally blew and the training session was over, the corporal went down on one knee and whistled to the little dog. The dog pricked up his ears. The soldier whistled again and the dog sat up and wagged his tiny docked tail. Then the soldier patted his thigh and smiled.

Sensing no danger, the chestnut-brown pup scampered across the field, his tongue lolling happily from one side of his mouth. As soon as he reached the soldier he gambolled onto the grass and rolled over onto his back, presenting his soft white tummy for a tickle.

The corporal laughed and obliged. 'Where did you come from, little fella?' he asked as he rubbed the dog's soft fur. 'Why, you ain't wearing a collar! You're pretty darn scrawny too. I reckon you must be a stray. Am I right?'

The dog answered by springing to his feet, putting his paws up on the soldier's knees and licking his face eagerly.

Noticing the dog's short, stubby tail, which all this time hadn't stopped wagging furiously, the corporal announced, 'Well, I'm going to call you Stubby, and if you stick with me, I'll make sure you get well fed. What do you think about that?'

As if he understood every word, Stubby barked and barked until the soldier scooped him up and took him into the barracks.

From that day forward, the corporal and the dog were rarely parted. Stubby would take himself off while his master was training and return in time for a meal each night as the sun was going down. Then he would curl up underneath the corporal's bed and sleep soundly until dawn.

Stubby was happier than he had ever been, and the corporal was glad to have a companion, for he had been missing his farmstead home where his ma and pa always had plenty of sheep dogs around to help control their cattle and to guard the property at night.

So when his training was over and his troop was called to action, the corporal could not bear the thought of being parted from his faithful new friend. With the help of his fellow soldiers, the corporal smuggled Stubby on board the ship that was to carry them across the ocean to France.

The men almost succeeded in keeping the little dog's presence a secret. However, one night, when the ship was not far from the French coast, a staff sergeant came into Corporal Conroy's cabin for an off-the-cuff inspection and spotted the little dog bunked up with his master.

All the men in the cabin were immediately woken as the air turned blue and the staff sergeant demanded to know whose dog it was and what was going on.

Still groggy from sleep, the startled corporal struggled to think of an answer that would calm his superior officer. He stammered and stuttered. But words were not needed, for Stubby jumped down from the bunk, sat firmly and obediently at the shiny toe-caps of the staff sergeant's highly-polished boots, and raised his right paw to his eye.

The staff sergeant went quiet. He blinked twice, not believing his own eyes. Then he started to laugh. 'Well, blow me down if the little critter isn't giving me a salute,' he chuckled. 'Looks like your dog's better trained that you, Corporal Conroy!'

So Stubby had managed to melt even the hardest of hearts, and even though Corporal Conroy was ordered to perform extra duties for smuggling an unauthorised animal on board, the staff sergeant allowed the clever dog to stay, on the strict instructions that he didn't get in the way.

Only days later, the corporal and his troop experienced their first taste of combat, thrown in at the deep end at the Battle of Malmaison where they were tasked with helping the French to recapture the ridge at Chemin des Dames. For many of the soldiers, most of them young and barely out of school, this was a terrifying time.

The mud in the trenches turned rust-red with blood, as one after another the young soldiers fell. Everywhere he looked, Corporal Conroy could see friends lying wounded or dying under heavy artillery fire, and the noise of the exploding shells and machine guns rattled his eardrums and made him cry out loud for mercy.

Yet amid all the chaos, Stubby remained calm. He was not afraid.

Anxious to keep his little companion safe, the corporal taught Stubby to duck down behind the sandbags. He was surprised how quickly Stubby caught on. He learned so quickly, in fact, that he was soon the first to duck as each new wave of German bombardment came crashing down upon them.

'I reckon that dog of yours can hear the shells coming before we can,' remarked the staff sergeant, before bellowing down the trench, 'Listen men, keep an eye on Stubby here. He'll warn you of incoming fire.'

It wasn't just enemy bullets and shells that Stubby was able to detect coming. He was also the first to know when there was poison gas in the air. His sensitive little nose would twitch as he caught the first whiff of it on the breeze and he would immediately begin to bark, buying the soldiers vital time to pull on their gas masks, or start up their Ayrton fans to blow the fatal fumes away.

The stories of Stubby's amazing abilities spread rapidly from one man to the next, from trench to trench. By day, stories of the clever little dog were shared between friends as they lay, side by side, at their gun posts. By night, whispers of his brave deeds were passed around, as the men huddled together around a flickering candle. The soldiers wrote about Stubby, too, in their postcards and letters home to their families and loved ones, and the tales of the dog's achievements became more exaggerated and more impressive by the day.

There was the story of how, one night, Stubby woke up while the corporal and all the other men in the trench were sleeping. It was said that the dog had heard something moving, so he crept through the mud in the bottom of trench without making a sound, and peeped around the corner. Sure enough, there was a German spy, creeping about under cover of darkness, scouting for maps and clues as to his enemy's battle plans.

The soldiers told how Stubby crouched down low on his tummy and crawled right up to the German. Then, with a growl, he sprang up and bit the soldier hard on the back of his thigh. The soldier cried out in alarm as the pain shot through his leg, waking the slumbering Americans nearby. They grappled the spy to the ground and took his weapon, but even then the determined little dog would not let go of his prey. Only when he saw Corporal Conroy approaching did he relax his jaws and release the petrified German.

And so the tales of the little dog's heroic deeds multiplied, until he had fought in as many as eighteen battles, and had been injured many times. He even received a wound stripe, like a real soldier, after being hurt by a wooden splinter that had stuck in his side.

There are those who said that Stubby met President Wilson, while he was visiting his troops in France, and shook the President's hand with his paw. Others claimed that Stubby was the first dog ever to have been made an honorary sergeant.

Which of these tales are true and which are legend, we may never be sure, but we do know that both Stubby and his master, Corporal Conroy, survived the Great War and returned home safely to America.

Once there, Stubby was rewarded with medals for his bravery. Now a nationwide hero, he travelled from state to state, the star of countless war parades, with Corporal Conroy always at his side. Wherever they went, the pair drew in the crowds, as people clamoured to see the little stray dog who had become a sergeant.

When the excitement began to die down, it was time for Corporal Conroy to turn his mind to their future. He headed for Georgetown University in Washington DC to study law, taking his canine friend with him.

Proud to have such a famous war hero on campus, the students quickly adopted Stubby as their football team mascot, an honour which the dog appeared to relish, for at the half-time hooter he could often be seen nudging a football around the field with his nose as the crowds cheered.

Stubby grew old, happy and content and ever loyal to his friend and master the corporal. One evening soon after, on 4 April 1926, Stubby climbed into Corporal Conroy's lap one last time. There, in his master's arms, he fell into a deep peaceful sleep, dreaming of a Great War from which this time, he would never return.

11: The Soldier and the Donkey

As the Austrian Archduke was shot, and Europe hurtled towards war, children in back alleys, snickets and ginnels all over England were bouncing balls and skipping rope while singing the following verse:

When the moon shines bright on Charlie Chaplin
His boots are cracking, for want of blacking
And his little baggy trousers they want mending
Before we send him to the Dardanelles.

Charlie Chaplin was a famous comic actor. This jolly rhyme that carried his name foretold the dark clouds of war that were gathering, for although Charlie never had to leave his home in Switzerland, a whole generation of British men were soon marching away.

The Dardanelles is a narrow strip of sea in Turkey which separates Europe from Asia. Forming its north coast is the Gallipoli Peninsula, the site of a bloody Allied campaign against Turkey that lasted from 25 April 1915 to 9 January 1916. The Allies hoped to win control of the Dardanelles and the capital of the Ottoman Empire, Constantinople (now called Istanbul), as this would have given them a safe sea route through from the Aegean Sea to the Black Sea and the coast of Russia. However, the campaign failed and many thousands of soldiers on both sides were left dead, either from the fighting or from disease.

The first wave of the Allied attack on the Gallipoli Peninsula, on 25 April 1915, involved landing troops from Australia and New Zealand on a beach now known as Anzac Cove. ANZAC stands for Australian and New Zealand Army Corps. Among the Australian soldiers was an Englishman named John 'Jack' Simpson, born John Kirkpatrick, whose story has become an ANZAC legend. Here follows a retelling of that tale...

There was once a boy called John Kirkpatrick Simpson. He was born in 1892 in South Shields, a coastal town in County Durham, which lies in the part of England known today as Tyne and Wear.

Although he was christened John, most people called the boy Jack. Jack loved animals, and as a schoolboy he would spend the long, sunny days of his summer holidays working with the donkeys who gave tourists and holiday-makers rides on the beach. Life was good and Jack was happy. But when he was just seventeen, his father died and his family's fortunes changed. Jack soon found himself looking for a new life.

Having a taste for adventure, Jack decided to become a seaman, and he travelled all the way to the other side of the world – all the way, in fact, to Australia. Jack liked this exotic new country so much that he decided to take a risk and, along with a dozen of his fellow seamen, jumped ship, going absent without leave, never to return.

Jack found himself a job as a labourer and there, thousands of miles from his South Shields home, he might well have stayed had he not heard the news, five years later, of a Great War which had begun back home in Europe. Anxious to do his part, Jack signed up with the Australian Air Force, using the new, shorter name of John Simpson, thinking that he might soon be on his way back home to Blighty or, at least, to nearby France.

But that was not to be, for Jack – now John – was destined for a more distant battlefield. Assigned to the

3rd Field Ambulance Brigade, John was tasked with being a stretcher-bearer.

If he thought that the job of a stretcher-bearer would be easy, John had a nasty surprise. On 25 April 1915, his brigade landed on the beaches of the Gallipoli coast. As they disembarked on the sands of the tiny Anzac Cove, John and his comrades were met with a daunting and difficult climb up steep cliffs and, to their horror, they quickly came under fire from the enemy troops, hidden among the dunes.

John was a quick thinker. With men falling all around him, he immediately set to work. At the camp on the beach, he loaded his empty stretcher with water supplies and hurried up the steep pathways to quench the thirst of the Australian troops as they fought their way inland. Then, water supplies distributed, he would swiftly load a wounded soldier onto his now empty stretcher and carry him back to the beach, to a safe place, where he could be cared for.

But there were too many men injured and too few stretchers, and John and his fellow ambulance workers were forced to carry the wounded soldiers on their backs.

That was, until John spotted a donkey wandering across the sand. Remembering the skills he had learned as a boy on the beach in South Shields, John wrapped a bandage around the donkey's nose, forming a makeshift rein, and led it towards the fighting to collect his next wounded soldier.

Amid the chaos and the noise of the battlefield, John and the donkey became firm friends. John named the donkey Duffy, and for the next three and a half weeks, they trudged back and forth from the beach, day and night, dodging enemy fire as they climbed up and down Shrapnel Gully and the Monash Valley, carrying water on the way and wounded men on the way back.

No matter how hard his task, John never became downhearted. As long as he had his faithful companion Duffy by his side, he could be heard singing and whistling as he went on his way, taking no heed of the bullets that whizzed past him and the shells that exploded all around.

Then, on the morning of 19 May, as he was leading Duffy down through Monash Valley with an injured man on the donkey's back, the determined and courageous John – just 22 years of age – was hit and killed by a bullet from a Turkish machine gun.

That might have been the end of the tale, but his faithful friend Duffy had other ideas. The brave little donkey was not to be stopped. He knew what his master and friend would have wanted him to do. And so he continued down the well-worn track, carrying the wounded man sprawled across his back all the way to safety.

The story of a soldier with a clever donkey as his companion, who had together saved so many lives, spread through the Australian army and became a symbol of the bravery that so many Allied soldiers displayed at Gallipoli. Some versions of the story give the donkey a different name: sometimes Abdul, sometimes Murphy, even sometimes Queenie. And there are those who say that on his last fateful journey, he was carrying not one but two wounded soldiers back from the front line. But whichever is the true version of the tale, there is no doubt that John 'Jack' Simpson Kirkpatrick's story made him a legend on both sides of the globe.

Today, if you visit South Shields, you can see for yourself one of the six statues that have been raised in honour of the legendary John Simpson. But to see the other five, you would have to follow in John's footsteps, and travel to Australia, all the way round to the other side of the world.

12: The Spooky Submarine

The waters of the North Atlantic are awash with stories of ghost ships, jinxed vessels and unexplained sinkings and explosions. The tale of the German U-boat or submarine that follows is one of the nastiest and most mysterious. It involves a vessel known as UB-65. It was originally believed that UB-65 sank off the coast of Ireland on 10 July 1918. However in 2004, an underwater archaeological survey proved that the vessel had actually sunk four days later, off Cornwall.

During the Great War, the German Admiralty used a shipbuilding yard in Bruges in Belgium to build their fleet of U-boats, the submarines that were to terrify the British supply convoys bringing precious supplies to Britain.

In 1917, a brand new U-boat was in the dock. Her construction was nearly complete when Jacques, a dockyard worker, paused in his brushing. He had been distracted by a shiny coin, a franc that had been dropped by a welder. With his eyes fixed downward, Jacques failed to notice the steel girder being swung into position on a steel strop from a crane above. The end of the girder hit the hapless cleaner square on the temple, killing him stone dead. As the girder dropped neatly into position in the superstructure of the sub, some of his blood and skull went with it, and so Jacques became the first victim of that jinxed U-boat, the UB-65.

In days gone by, when employers were not so bound to health and safety regulations, losing a labourer or two during the construction of a great vessel like the UB-65 was not that rare. So work did not stop with the loss of poor Jacques, and just one month later the UB-65 was launched for her first sea trials. In the engine room the poor souls with their rags and long-spouted oil cans spluttered, retched and vomited as the engine room filled with fumes. Three of these unfortunate souls collapsed onto the rough steel floor and expired. They had suffocated in the smog.

UB-65 had now claimed four lives – a jinx indeed.

Of course, the German Admiralty kept news of these tragedies under wraps, not wishing to give the English Navy the chance of using it for propaganda. And even though the U-boat's captain knew that his crew were getting jumpy, he closed the hatches for the sub's first dive.

However, just to make sure all was safe and secure, the captain sent a reliable sailor forward for an outside inspection of the hatches. On a day of flat calm as it was, this was a normal procedure. Yet inexplicably, this experienced sailor stepped off the vessel and was swept away in the wash.

UB-65 had now claimed five lives.

And the death toll did not stop rising. On that very same dive, UB-65 struck the sea bed and the briny water seeped in. For hours, the captain tried and failed to raise his vessel. Then, just as the captain was about to give up, the sub rose mysteriously to the surface.

The crew sailed the UB-65 back to Bruges for repairs and arming, thinking that their luck had changed. But during the arming process, a torpedo warhead exploded, killing six and taking the sub's death toll to eleven.

Among the sailors killed in the torpedo blast was the Second Lieutenant. An ambitious young man, he had often stood, arms folded, on the prow of the vessel, enjoying making himself appear important.

The crew thought that they had seen the last of him, but that very night some of the sailors swore that they saw the Second Lieutenant standing, once again, on the prow, his arms folded. Meanwhile others saw him walking in the corridor, leading from the torpedo bay.

The Imperial Navy took the mysterious incidents on the UB-65 so seriously that they had the submarine exorcised by a priest. But their efforts were in vain.

During the crew's next tour of duty, a gunner went mad, the Chief Engineer broke his leg and one sailor committed suicide – and before every one of these tragedies, crew members reported seeing the Second Lieutenant, standing with his arms folded on the prow of the vessel, keeping an eye on things.

Given her record, it was inevitable that the UB-65 would meet a sorry end, although nobody thought it would be quite as strange as it was.

On 14 July 1918, the UB-65 was drifting off the Cornish coast near Padstow when the skipper of an American submarine, the L2, spotted the vessel with the ghostly Second Lieutenant on her prow. As he watched, wondering what the officer was doing, an explosion tore the German U-boat apart from stem to stern.

As the white smoke and mist dispersed, the Second Lieutenant on the prow gave one final salute as the wreck of the spooky submarine dipped beneath the Atlantic waves for the last time.

13: THE BRAVE NURSE

If you were asked to name someone who could be described as a 'living legend', who would it be? You might immediately think of someone you adore, admire or respect, such as a pop star, a movie star or a footballer. Perhaps you would choose someone incredibly brave, adventurous or clever, such as Malala Yousafzai, Bear Grylls or Professor Stephen Hawking. Alternatively, perhaps someone would spring to mind who is legendary for a negative reason, such as a notorious criminal or an unpopular political leader. Will the person you chose be remembered for decades to come? Will people still be telling stories about them in fifty, sixty, even one hundred years' time?

Consider which people from the past have managed to attain that legendary status. Whose actions and achievements have not only earned them a place in the history books, but have led to stories about them being passed down from one generation to the next? Now pick one of these people, and consider how much of their story you know to be true. Can every detail about their life be proven as fact? You may find that their story has been changed, enhanced and edited along the way. Yet perhaps that is what makes legends so interesting. They all start with some element of truth, but they can evolve and grow so that each retelling is fresh, exciting and new.

We should not be surprised how many legends have their roots in the First World War. In those tumultuous years of 1914–1918, there were thousands upon thousands of people whose actions and bravery deserve respect and admiration. We will never know all of their stories, but one person whose story has earned a place in legend is British nurse, Edith Cavell (4 December 1865–12 October 1915). Edith did not become famous until after her death, and although no one can deny that she deserved her legendary status, it is quite possible that her story would never have become so well known had the British Government not chosen to champion her as a war hero.

The following tale is inspired by Edith's life story...

On a cold December morning in 1865, a baby girl was born in the small Norfolk village of Swardeston. Her father, Frederick, was the vicar of the village church, and her mother, Louisa Sophia, was the daughter of Frederick's housekeeper.

Frederick and Louisa adored their baby girl. They christened her Edith, and looked forward to the day when they could settle with their new daughter in the brand new vicarage which was soon to be their home.

Frederick was a generous man – some may say foolishly so – for the money which was being spent on the new vicarage, next to the church, was coming from his own pocket. No matter, he always said, that his own family had to go without some luxuries, it was right and proper that they should set a good example and be charitable towards others.

The baby Edith thrived and grew into a healthy, active young girl. More Cavell children followed, and the well-behaved Edith was a perfect big sister to her three siblings, Florence, Lilian and little John, whom they all called Jack.

Louisa loved her children so much, that when they became old enough for schooling, she could not bear to part with them and announced that she would teach them at home. So all four children would spend their weekdays around the large circular table in the vicarage's library, learning about far away countries, reading about the wonders of the natural world, studying art, music and the sciences, and of course, learning how to read and write and do their sums. At the weekends they would spill outdoors and play happily together in the vicarage gardens. But the best days of all, were those when their father wasn't busy in the parish. Then he would join in their games and even dress up in a bear costume and chase them around the house.

Within this nurturing, caring environment, Edith grew into a confident and enterprising young teenager. No teenage rebellion for her; rather she channeled her energies into positive things, such as helping her mother in the Sunday School and raising money for a new Sunday School room.

At last, the time came for Edith to leave home and start to find her own way in life. At sixteen, she waved goodbye to her mother and father, and to Florence, Lilian and Jack, and headed off to boarding school.

Edith missed her home, but she was hungry to learn and she worked hard in all her lessons, showing herself to have a natural talent for French. She longed to be a teacher, so as soon as she had passed all her exams, she found a job as a governess.

Edith enjoyed her new role, and was pleased to be able to provide the same kind of love and affection to her young charges as she had received from her own parents. Yet she could not extinguish the burning desire for adventure that had sparked inside her in those happy days of home schooling alongside her brother and sisters. She wanted to learn more about the world, to expand her knowledge and become the best teacher she could be.

So when the generosity of a kind departed soul saw Edith inheriting a modest sum of money, she leapt at the opportunity for her first taste of travel and exploration. Heading for the snow-capped mountains and the lush green valleys of Austria and Bavaria, she travelled to some of Europe's most beautiful countries, soaking up the language and culture like a sponge.

It was on her travels that Edith first came upon a venture which was to change the course of her life. She visited a hospital whose doors were open to everyone, rich or poor, no matter what their background or status, and where all treatment was free. It was run by a man with the memorable name of Doctor Wolfenberg, and so impressed was Edith with his charitable approach to medicine, that not only did she decide to donate her remaining inheritance to the hospital, she also made up her mind that one day, she was going to become a nurse.

But with no more money to spend, Edith knew she must first return to work as a governess.

For five years, she cared for the children of a French-speaking Belgian family in the beautiful city of Brussels and became so fluent in French that it was difficult to tell her from the locals.

Although now a mature woman approaching thirty years of age, Edith still missed her home back in Norfolk and whenever she had time off, would return to the peace and tranquility of Swardeston and the beautiful vicarage with its moat. It was on one such summer break that Edith first fell in love. The object of her desire was her second cousin, Eddie.

But there was no time for their relationship to turn into anything stronger, for Edith's attention was soon diverted to her father, whose health was ailing. Terrified of losing him, Edith swapped her post in Brussels for a chair by her father's bedside and devoted her time to nursing him back to health. The joy of seeing her father getting better each day convinced Edith that nursing was really her destiny, and as soon as her father was strong enough, she headed for London and signed up at nursing school.

Once again, Edith was a star pupil, learning fast and working hard. She was not afraid of a challenge, no matter how big or small, even risking her own life to help the victims of a typhoid fever outbreak which was threatening to devastate the seaside town of Margate in Kent.

So fine a nurse did Edith show herself to be that she was soon back in Brussels, passing on her skills in a new nurses' training school. But life for Edith – and for the people of Belgium – was about to change again, and for the worse.

Edith's beloved father, Frederick, fell ill once more, and this time lost his battle for life. Then, in August 1914, while she was in Norfolk comforting her widowed mother, Edith heard the shocking news that Germany, under orders from its power-hungry Kaiser, had invaded Belgium.

The grief-stricken Louisa begged her daughter to stay in the relative safety of Britain but Edith, whose sense of duty was strong, knew that the teaching hospital now needed her more than ever, and she hurried back across the sea to Belgium.

If the German army had expected an easy passage through Belgium to France, it had a nasty surprise, for the people of Belgium, outraged at the invasion, put up a serious fight. Snipers lay in wait for the invaders to arrive, civilians poured into the streets when they did, and the fighting was bloody and merciless. The German soldiers' response was even more ferocious and in a desperate attempt to maintain control, they swore to take ten Belgian lives for every German soldier lost.

The wounded and the dying poured into Edith's hospital which had now become a Red Cross station and, remembering the neutral approach of her mentor, Doctor Wolfenberg, she refused to turn anyone away. Man, woman or child, patients on both sides of the conflict lay next to one another and benefited from her care.

But despite the Belgians' best efforts, Brussels fell after only a few days of fighting, and one after the next Edith's nurses returned to England. Only Edith and one faithful assistant remained, determined to care for the wounded and the sick, whatever their allegiance.

Aware of the dangerous situation she was placing herself in, Edith put pen to paper and wrote a letter to send home to England.

My darling mother and family,
If you open this, it will be because that which we

fear has now happened, and Brussels has fallen into the hands of the enemy. They are very near now and it is doubtful if the Allied armies can stop them. We are prepared for the worse. I shall think of you to the last, and you may be sure we shall do our duty here and die as women of our race should die. God bless you and keep you safe.

One night that autumn, when everything was quiet in the ward and all the patients had settled into an uneasy sleep, Edith heard a noise in the grounds outside her window. Stepping into the back garden, her heart beating loudly in her chest as she peered into the dark, Edith came face to face with two disheveled British soldiers. On the point of exhaustion, the men told Edith how they had become separated from their battalion in the retreat from Mons. Lost and hungry, they were now stranded in enemy territory, desperately trying to make their way home.

Taking pity on her countrymen, Edith gave the men food and water and hid them in her quarters. For the next fourteen days, they remained there in secrecy, recovering from their ordeal, while Edith sought help.

We know by now that when Edith put her mind to something, she made it happen. Despite the danger, she joined an underground network of forgers, safe houses and guides which could furnish the two soldiers with the money, identity papers and maps they needed to make an escape north out of Belgium and across the flat fields, canals and dykes of Holland to the coast.

The two lucky survivors from Mons became the first of more than two hundred Allied soldiers who were provided with a safe passage home thanks to Edith's courage and tenacity. She was well aware that she and her fellow conspirators were at risk of arrest should any of them be discovered. She knew, too, that the soldiers she was hiding would be shot if caught. Yet she pressed on, each escape becoming more risky than the last as it became harder and harder to avoid the inquisitive eyes of the Germans.

Edith told no one of her secret activities. She sewed all incriminating paperwork safely inside a cushion in her room and always held her nerve, even when the Germans suspected that she was up to something and carried out a search of the clinic. While Edith calmly showed the soldiers around, her latest charge – a Belgian collaborator – crept out of the back garden unseen.

But Edith's luck was running out, for on 31 July 1915, the German soldiers came back to search the clinic again and this time, when they left, they took Edith with them, her hands bound. Whether they had been tipped off, or whether they had seen Edith acting suspiciously, they did not say. All her captors did tell her was that she was not alone: two others involved in her scheme had also been taken prisoner and they, the captors lied, had confessed all. Poor Edith, who believed what she was being told, accepted defeat and admitted her part.

It took just ten weeks for the Germans to bring Edith to trial and while pleas for her release came from as far away as America and Spain, the British Government remained silent, fearing their intervention would anger the Germans and do Edith more harm than good.

All alone in the dock, Edith's only defence for aiding the Allied soldiers was that, had she not helped them, they would have been shot. To her German accusers, this was no defence at all, and Edith was sentenced to be executed the very next day.

The last friendly face that Edith saw before she faced the firing squad came to her that night in the form of an English chaplain. Finding her calm, free of bitterness and resigned to her fate, the chaplain took communion with Edith, then they quietly sang 'Abide With Me'. Holding back the tears, Edith gave the chaplain a prayer book, asking that he honour her last wish that it be taken to her cousin back in Swardeston. Only after he left the room did the chaplain glance inside and see that Edith had dedicated the book to her one and only sweetheart, sending her darling Eddie her love.

Edith Cavell and her two fellow conspirators were executed not long after dawn on 12 October 1915. There are those who say that that the men in the firing squad could not bear to shoot such a kind and gentle soul, and fired wide. There are those who say that before the guns fired, Edith fainted and was put to death instead by a single pistol shot, fired by a German officer. Others say that one of the gunmen threw down his rifle in protest and was himself shot alongside Edith for his disobedience. There is, of course, also the possibility that nothing out of the ordinary happened at all. But whatever the details of Edith's final moments, her body was hurriedly buried close to the firing range and her grave marked with a simple wooden cross.

Edith's life had been cut short, but the effects of it lived on, as news of her death sent ripples of anger around the world. In trying to make an example of the brave nurse, the Germans had given their enemies all the ammunition they needed for a powerful propaganda campaign. In this shocking story, the Germans were the evil villains and Edith was the perfect patriotic heroine – a symbol of bravery and courage.

So important was Edith's legacy considered to be, that when the war was finally over, special arrangements were made to return her body to Britain where she could be laid to rest in her beloved church in Swardeston. To mark her life, a memorial was held in her honour at Westminster Abbey, with Queen Alexandra and Princess Victoria in the congregation alongside nurses from all over the world. And in the spirit of Edith's sense of charity, The Cavell Nurses' Trust was set up in her name, to provide rest homes for retired nurses.

Edith never wanted fame and she never set out to become a martyr. But through her actions, her kindness, her bravery and her courage, she nonetheless became a true legend of the First World War.

14: THE CHRISTMAS TRUCE

The temporary truce which was called in the trenches in the Christmas of 1914 is well known thanks to the letters and diaries of the soldiers who were part of it. However, for those lucky enough to return home, the happenings of that Christmas would have been told to families and friends not as a series of facts but as a story... because that's what people do, quite naturally. Here is our version of that Christmas 1914 tale.

In December 1914, the soldiers of the King, under the command of General Haig, were locked in battle with the troops of the Kaiser on a long battle front, sometimes in France, more often in Belgium.

This was especially sad as many of the brave young men who had joined up had done so believing that the war would be all over by Christmas. But instead, at the blast of an officer's whistle, thousands of them found themselves going 'over the top' from their trenches, only to be scythed down by a hail of bullets from across No Man's Land, in the attempt to gain a minute piece of territory that would often revert back to the opposition in battle the following day.

Far away, in the peace of his office in the Vatican City, Pope Benedict XV suggested a temporary hiatus in the war for the celebration of Christmas.

His proposal was not well received by the high-ranking German and British officers who sat around the large circular tables of their respective command centres. They had worked hard to get their men addicted to the adrenaline of battle and so they had no appetite for the Pope's festive truce.

Yet in spite of the reluctance of the generals and the politicians, as Christmas drew nearer and the men all along the trenches began to receive parcels from loved ones at home, the Christmas spirit was growing.

A rash of tiny fir trees had broken out in No Man's Land. Whenever they could, the German soldiers would reach over the top of their trenches, wrench up the little trees and re-plant them in piles of earth marking the edge of their trench. Then, on Christmas Eve, they illuminated the trees with candles.

Fifty yards opposite, across the shell holes and abandoned dead bodies strewn across No Man's Land, soldiers in a Bedfordshire regiment paused to open their parcels from home.

Among them were Tommy and Billy, two mates who had at met at trials for Luton Town FC before going together to the army office to sign up. Tommy had been sent a knitted blanket, a fruit cake and some cigarettes, or 'coffin nails' as they called them. Billy was amazed to discover that his father had sent him a caser – a brown, flattened, leather football filled with a pink rubber bladder with the nozzle pointing through the lace holes. Tommy and the other soldiers pulled Billy's leg. Why would his dad think he would need such a gift?

Ignoring their jibes, Billy set about blowing the ball up, and used a small piece of twig to seal the tube. As no officers were watching, Billy and Tommy started a game of keepy-uppy.

They had just finished their game when they heard an outbreak of singing from the German trench.

Stille nacht,
Heilige nacht...

The English soldiers responded:

Silent night,
Holy night...

The two nations were singing the same carol to each other, in the middle of a war.

Then, following a friendly – if confused – interchange of shouts, soldiers on both sides climbed out of their trenches, carrying not guns but spades. After some brief and rather formal handshakes, they set about respectfully burying the dead who had been lying in No Man's Land for weeks, if not months.

When he climbed out of his trench, Billy could not resist taking along his new Christmas present. The brown leather caser caught the eye of a German infantryman called Gerhart, who, prior to the war, had played as goalkeeper for Bayern Munich. Straight away, Gerhart suggested a game of *fußball*.

Up until that point, the soldiers on both sides had kept their metal helmets on, removing them only briefly for the burials of their dead. Now all the helmets were off, and two pairs of them were placed on the ground to delineate goals.

Stripped of their protective headwear, this was to the soldiers no longer just a game of football, it was also a game of trust.

Tommy dribbled down the wing before centring the ball to Billy who was just about to score, when Gerhart screamed, 'Offside!' The German seized the ball and booted it downfield to a team member who had a tap in.

And so the game continued, until the precious ball was accidentally booted into a roll of barbed wire where, with a hissing sound, it expired. With the game brought to a sad and premature end, the two teams shook hands and returned to their respective trenches.

Just a few minutes later, following a sharp blast from an officer's whistle, and the crash of a whizz-bang shell, the truce was over and the two sides were at war again.

Billy's first shot over the parapet winged Gerhart and he couldn't resist shouting, 'That wasn't offside, was it?' He knew it was a cheap line, but it created a burst of laughter from both trenches.

Sadly, this was the last social exchange that those two groups of young men would have for a further four years, for the war raged on until 11 November 1918.

As for the score in the football match... well, it can be argued that that wasn't settled for fifty years, until 1966 at Wembley Stadium.

THE FIRST FRIENDLY

The pitch was all cratered and muddy,
Home-made ball not really round,
The goalposts were two pair of rifles
Stuck bayonet end in the ground.

The supporters all mixed in together
And they cheered no matter who scored
And nobody cared who was winning
Because footie's a game, not a war.

The final whistle was shellfire
So both sides, scattering, ran
Back to their own line of trenches

Each end of No-Man's Land.

Kevin McCann

For my Grandad, Gunner Edward Salter (L3004), Royal Artillery (1914–17), honourably discharged.

About the Authors

Taffy Thomas MBE trained as a Literature and Drama teacher at Dudley College of Education. He founded and directed the legendary folk theatre company, Magic Lantern, and the rural community arts company, Charivari. After a stroke, aged just 36, he turned back to storytelling as self-imposed speech therapy.

Taffy has a repertoire of more than 300 stories and tales collected mainly from traditional oral sources, and is now the most experienced English storyteller. In the 2001 New Year Honours List he was awarded the MBE for services to storytelling and charity. In October 2009 Taffy accepted the honorary position of the first Laureate for Storytelling. He is currently Artistic Director of Tales in Trust, the Northern Centre for Storytelling, in Grasmere. He tours nationally and internationally working in both entertainment and education and is a patron of the Society for Storytelling. In 2013, Taffy was selected as Outstanding Male Storyteller in the British Awards for Storytelling Excellence.

www.taffythomas.co.uk

Helen Watts is a writer, editor and publisher. Her experience includes magazine and book publishing, and she has worked for some of the biggest and best publishing houses in the UK, including Scholastic and Heinemann Educational. For ten years, Helen was Editor of the Literacy Time magazine, after which she founded The Literacy Club, through which she published magazines and books including the paperback collection by Taffy Thomas, *Taffy's Coat Tales*.

Helen's first historical fiction novel for teenagers and young adults, *One Day In Oradour* (A&C Black) has been nominated for the 2014 CILIP Carnegie Medal for an outstanding book for children. Her second novel for A&C Black, *No Stone Unturned*, will be published in 2014.

www.helenwattsauthor.com

Acknowledgements

'We Must Not Forget' by George Harrison, © George Harrison 2013, first published here, reproduced by permission of the author.

'Strange Meeting' by Wilfred Owen (1893–1918).

'The Moon Shines Bright on Charlie Chaplin', song lyrics, traditional.

'It's A Long, Long Way To Tipperary' by Jack Judge (1872–1938) and Harry Williams, written in 1912.

'The First Friendly' by Kevin McCann, text copyright © Kevin McCann, 2010, first published in *The World at Our Feet* (Macmillan, 2010), reproduced by permission of the author.

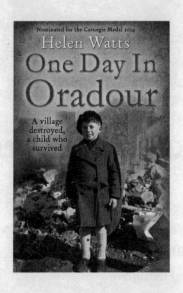

One Day in Oradour
Helen Watts

On a hot summer afternoon in 1944, SS troops wiped
out an entire French village. 644 men, women and children
died that day. Just one child survived. This book tells the
story of what happened in Oradour, and imagines what drove
both the SS officer who ordered the massacre, and
the seven-year-old boy who escaped it.

£6.99   ISBN 9781408182017

Nominated for the Carnegie Medal 2014